This Little Tiger book belongs to:

____

____

____

Remembering Pat O'Hanlon
MM

In memory of Mum and Dad,
and with love to Gerry for
all her support
MO

LITTLE TIGER PRESS
An imprint of Magi Publications
1 The Coda Centre, 189 Munster Road, London SW6 6AW
www.littletigerpress.com

First published in Great Britain 2004

Printed in Dubai by Oriental Press

ISBN 1 85430 967 6

A CIP catalogue record for this book
is available from the British Library

10 9 8 7 6 5 4 3 2 1

Foley and Jem

Mary Murphy   Mark Oliver

LITTLE TIGER PRESS
LONDON

Jem was just like any dog:
handsome, brave and full-hearted.
He lived with his owner, Foley.
They were very happy.
Jem loved Foley,
and Foley loved Jem.

Foley loved Jem, and he also loved the stars. He read about planets and the Universe and black holes. Sometimes he read a book about Earth, just for Jem.

At night Foley watched the stars. Jem sat by him, his head in Foley's lap. He gazed at Foley, and Foley gazed at the stars.

"Good dog, good dog," Foley said, patting Jem's head.

Then things began to change. At Christmas Jem gave Foley a star on a string. Foley forgot to give anything to Jem.

"Sorry, Jem," he said.

Jem forgave him, just like any dog would.

All Foley thought about was going into space. Jem wasn't interested. Foley made plans and calculations. He worked hard.

It took him years to build it . . .

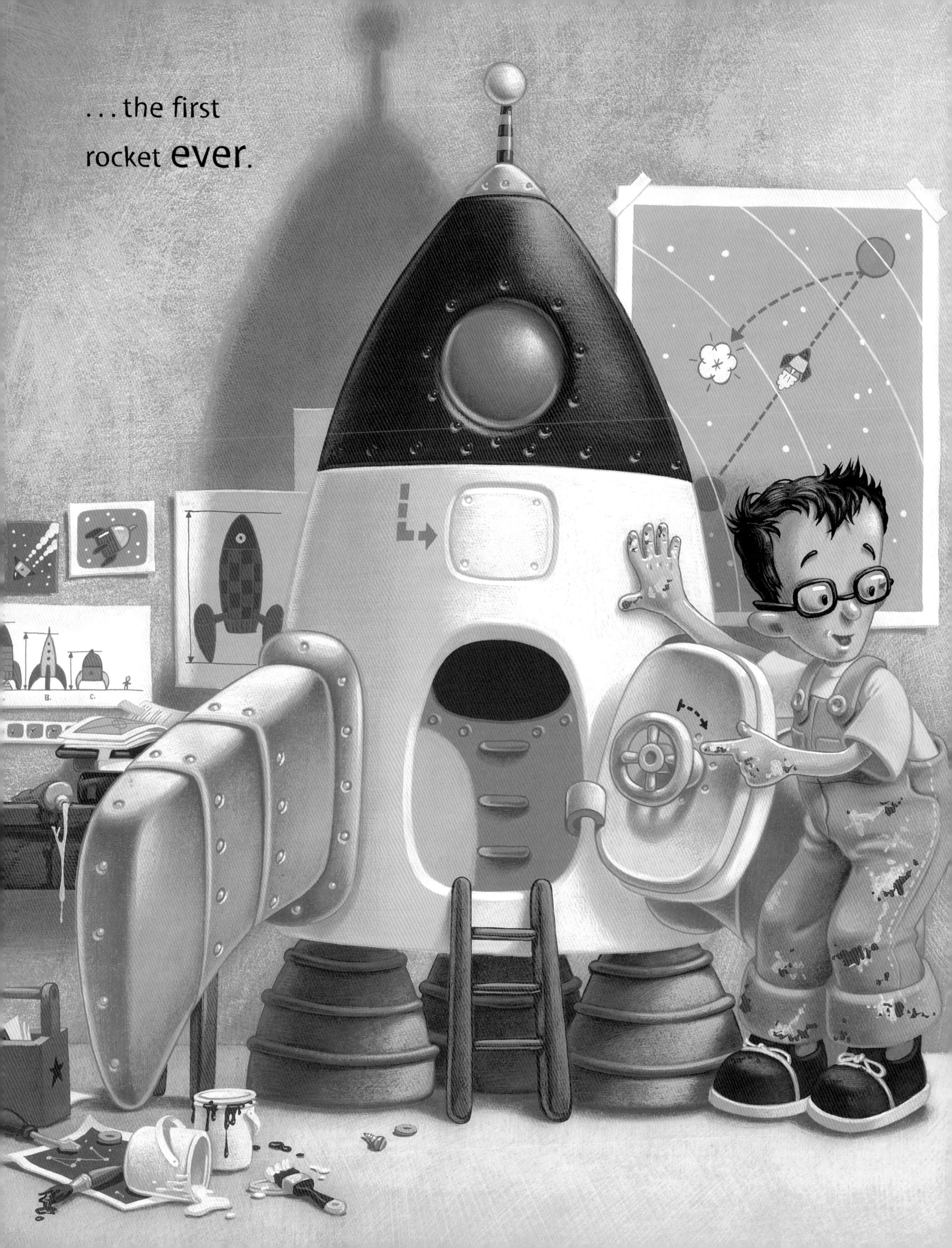

. . . the first
rocket **ever**.

Foley's rocket would go all the way into space and land on Mars.

"Isn't it fantastic, Jem?" said Foley. "Imagine exploring Mars!"

Foley had one worry. Would the rocket explode on the way back, when it met the Earth's atmosphere? He kept working and calculating.

"I wish I could go in the rocket, but I need to control things from Earth," said Foley. "You can go, Jem. You're clever, for a dog."

"I am not just a dog," said Jem, shocked. "I am your friend!"

But Foley did not understand dog language.

Foley made a special spacesuit for Jem. Jem learned all the rocket controls.

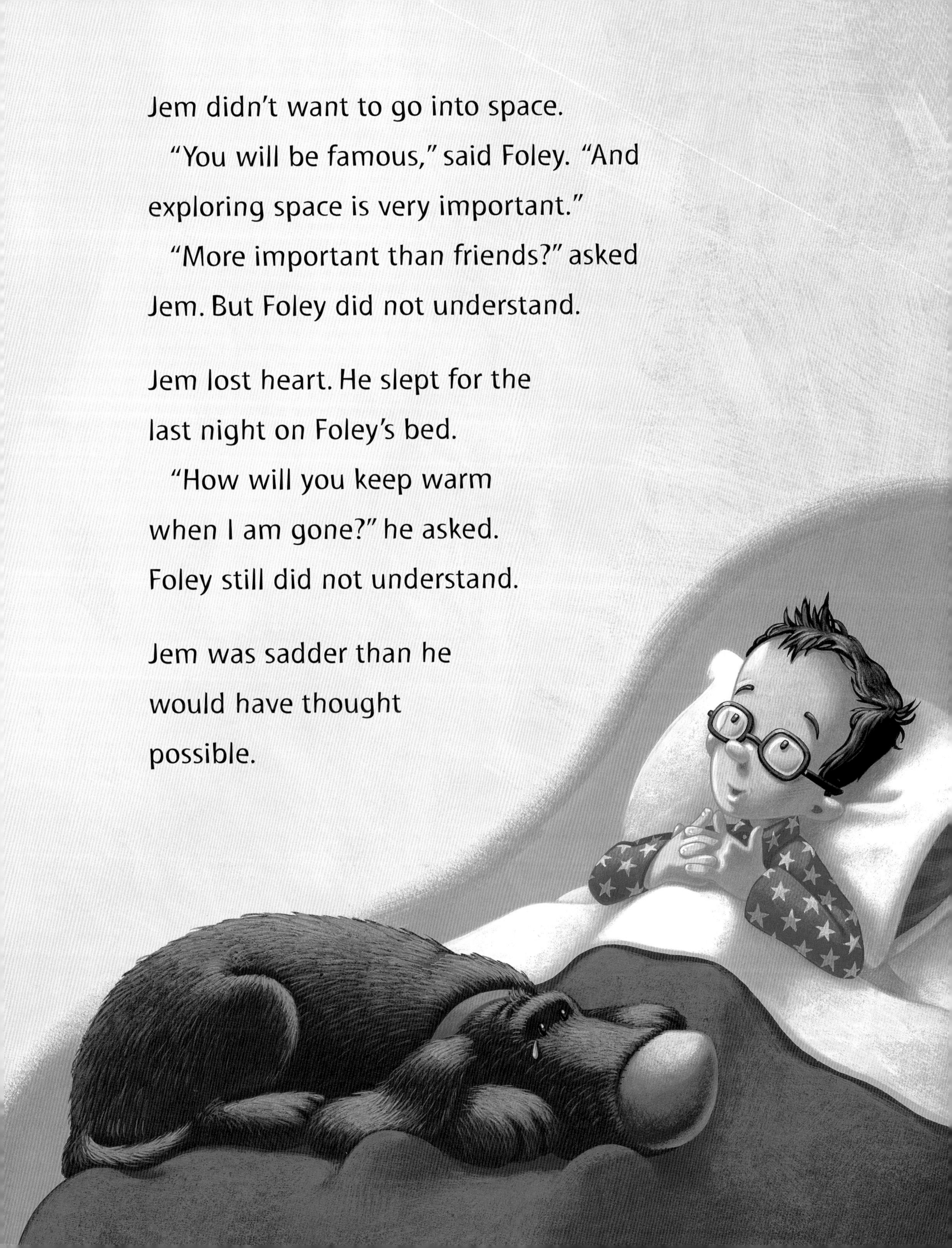

Jem didn't want to go into space.

"You will be famous," said Foley. "And exploring space is very important."

"More important than friends?" asked Jem. But Foley did not understand.

Jem lost heart. He slept for the last night on Foley's bed.

"How will you keep warm when I am gone?" he asked. Foley still did not understand.

Jem was sadder than he would have thought possible.

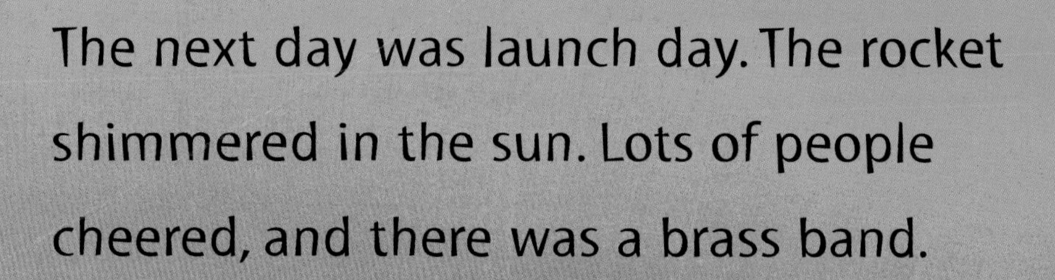

The next day was launch day. The rocket shimmered in the sun. Lots of people cheered, and there was a brass band.

The countdown started.

Ten! Nine! Eight!

"You're beautiful!" said Foley, to the rocket.

Seven! Six! Five!

Foley squinted to see Jem at the rocket window.

Four! Three!

"Goodbye, Jem," said Foley, suddenly sad.

Two! One!

The rocket rose
into the air.

"Goodbye, Earth!" cried Jem,
alone in the rocket.

Space felt cold and empty and lonely.
"But it's beautiful," said Jem, surprised.
"And interesting. No wonder Foley loves it."

He used the special camera to send
pictures back to Foley.

That night Foley thought of Jem and watched the sky.

"Good dog," he said, patting his knee where Jem's head usually rested. He felt a bony knee instead of a warm, silky head.

"Time for bed," said Foley.

The bed felt cold and empty and lonely.

Jem landed the rocket
safely on Mars. He sent a message:

ARRIVED SAFELY.

He did everything properly, just like any
dog would. Mars was rocks and cracks
and sand. Jem sent pictures to Foley.
"Not very interesting after all,"
Foley said.

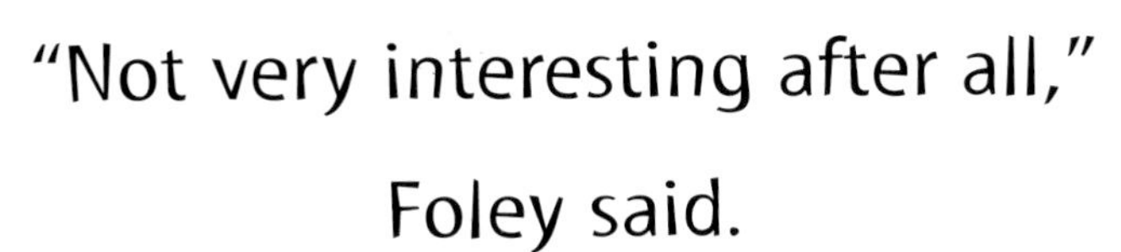

The next day Jem walked to the side
of Mars we can't see from Earth.

What a sight!

"Hello," said the Martians.

"Hello," said Jem. They understood each other.

"You are welcome, Earthling," they said.

Jem could breathe Martian air without his spacesuit. "This is even better than Earth!" he said.

Jem did not send any pictures to Foley that day.

The next day, Foley sent
a message to Jem.

I MISS YOU. PLEASE SEND PICTURE
OF YOUR FRIENDLY FACE. NO MORE
ROCKS AND CRACKS AND SAND.

Jem put on his spacesuit,
and sent this picture
and message.

I'M HAPPY HERE.
DON'T WORRY. WILL SEND
ROCKET BACK TOMORROW.

Jem sent the rocket back and
it did explode when it met the Earth's
atmosphere. It looked like a shooting star.

"Now I'll never see my friend again,"
said Foley. He looked at the photo.
"But at least he is happy
on Mars."

That was the end of the story for a while.

Then one night while Foley looked up at Mars, a little puppy came and sat beside him.

"Hello, little one," said Foley. "Have you nowhere to go? Will you stay with me?"

She stayed. Foley called her Judy, and looked after her. He didn't want to lose another friend. He loved her properly, and she loved him, just like any dog would.

And Jem? He really
was happy on Mars,
happier than he would
have thought possible.
Just like any dog
would be.

Take off with more books from Little Tiger Press!

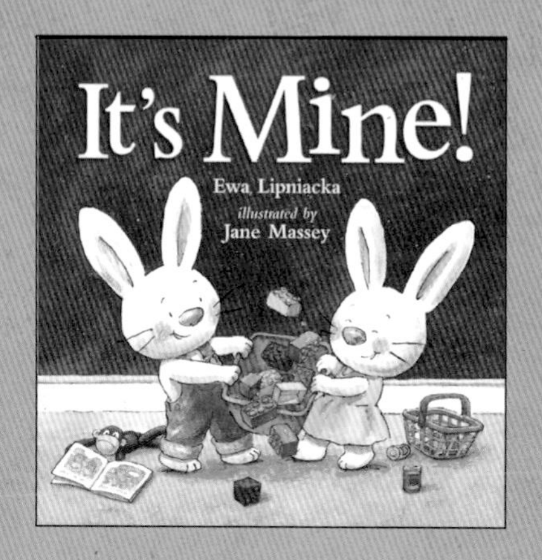

For information regarding
any of the above titles or for
our catalogue, please contact us:
Little Tiger Press, 1 The Coda Centre,
189 Munster Road, London SW6 6AW
Tel: 020 7385 6333 Fax: 020 7385 7333
E-mail: info@littletiger.co.uk www.littletigerpress.com